I'm Happy

I'm Happy

Halle Harty

Copyright © Halle Harty 2023

For my family and friends, who have helped me and supported me through everything.

Chapter 1
Nicole Jones

The noise in the cafeteria is ridiculous. I know that everyone is having their own conversations and all but sometimes it sounds like everyone is yelling. There always seems to be at least one fight going on, and it gets very loud very quick. That's why I don't understand why my friends and I sit in the cafeteria for lunch. And when I say friends, I really mean my family. My brother Austin is a year older than I am, and he is in eleventh grade. What may surprise many people is that we actually do hang out quite a bit. He was sitting across the table from me, but his hazel eyes were glued to his phone. His brown hair as usual looked messy, but I think it is because of his early morning football practice.

"Hey, what are you doing?" I asked him.

"I'm just reading this email from my coach," he told me.

"What's it about?" I asked.

"Just one of our games," he replied. He seemed a little nervous about whatever the email was, but I didn't want to pry too much.

"Hey guys!" Callie, our cousin, said enthusiastically as she sat down next to me. Her blue eyes looked excited, but that is just because she was happy and her eyes were not failing to show it. She had her dirty blond hair curled and a bit of light makeup. For being cousins, we don't really look that alike. We both got our hair and eye color from our dads, which make us look quite a bit different. While she had the lighter colors, I had brown hair and hazel eyes. We did both get our mom's face shape, but that is about where the similarities in appearance end. She and I were both in grade ten, but we only have one class together.

"Hey, how's it going?" I asked her, as if I couldn't already tell she was happy.

"Great!" she exclaimed. "My volleyball coach told me I get to start next weekend!"

"Congrats!" I said.

"Yeah, that's huge!" My brother joined in.

"What's huge?" Justin, our other cousin and Callie's brother, asked as he sat down.

"Coach said I will start next weekend!" Callie repeated.

"Hey, congrats!" he said. He and my brother are in the same boat as Callie and I. Justin has blonde hair and blue eyes like Callie, and Austin and I look pretty similar. They are both in eleventh grade but are pretty different people. My brother gets good grades, but he is super athletic and would much rather be playing sports. Justin is not super athletic, but he makes up for it in academics. He gets a close to perfect score on anything that he gets marked on, which I don't understand at all. This table is where my social circle ends, within the safety of my family. I have tried to make friends before but something my old 'friend' did lead to a falling out, and I have been terrified to try and make close friendships ever since. Callie had tried to get me to hang out with some girls from her volleyball team, but it felt forced and a little bit awkward. I like spending time with my family though. The only feeling I don't like is the one that I get every odd time that tells me they don't want to spend time with me. Even though I know it's not true, it's hard not to feel that way when the only people that hangout with you are your family and even they have other friend groups.

Chapter 2
Run

I was sitting in my room debating if I should go for a run when my brother walked in. "Hey," he said.

"Hi," I said.

"Are you free?"

"For what?"

"I don't know, I just feel like we haven't hung out in a while."

"Okay, do you want to go for a run?"

"Sure!"

"Okay meet me downstairs by the door in ten minutes," I said. I was a little excited. Austin left smiling. This might not seem like a big deal, but it was to me. He was right. We hadn't hung out outside of school in a while, because he was super busy. We actually like spending time with each other and after this year he only has one year before he moves away, so spending time with each other has become a priority. I changed my shirt and found my baseball cap and then went downstairs to put on my runners. Austin was already downstairs by the door with a huge smile on his face.

"Are you ready to go?" he asked me.

"Yes, just give me a second," I said, as I quickly put my shoes on.

"Mom, we're going for a run!" Austin yelled.

"Ok be back for dinner at 5:30!" Mom yelled back from the kitchen.

We were about halfway through the run, and we had been talking the entire time. It felt like forever since we had done this.

"There is one thing I will never understand about you," he said as soon as it got quiet.

"Oh, what's that?"

"You are athletic but refuse to be on a sports team. If you were, maybe you would have the opportunity to make friends."

"You know I've thought about it before, but it's really just not my thing. I like going for runs with you or by myself, and besides I like just hanging out with you, Justin, and Callie."

"Don't get me wrong. We love hanging out with you but just think about this for a second. In about 2 years Justin and I are gone and when we are gone you're going to be in senior year. I am not saying Callie doesn't like hanging out with you, and I am definitely not saying she will stop hanging out with you, but she might be busy. She is kind of a social butterfly, and you and I both know she has a lot of friends. We also know she likes almost every sport ever and once she gets into the senior level for high school sports, you have to be more committed. It wouldn't hurt if you at least tried to make some friends that aren't us."

"I know. It's just hard. You know that I have a hard time judging people's characters until it's too late."

"Nicole, you can't beat yourself up about that one time." We were almost home now.

"I really thought she was my friend, but she was just getting a bunch of info on me and then told it to all of her other friends. They still pick on me sometimes you know?"

"Like just her or all of her friends?"

"Every last one of them."

"Even the boyfriend I got into a fight with last year?"

"Especially him, but please don't get into another fight!"

"Ok I promise," he said. "Alright change of subject. You know how it's Callie's birthday next week?"

"Yeah of course I do!"

"Well the two of you are in grade 10, and it is her sixteenth birthday…"

"Ok, where's this going?"

"Well Justin was going to throw her a party, and he kind of asked us to both help and come."

"Ok what kind of party?"

"You know like an actual high school kind of party-"

"You know that's not my scene. I can help plan it, but I just don't think I can go to a party."

"But wouldn't it be fun to just try to go to a party? Plus I feel like Callie would be disappointed if you don't come," he argued.

"What if I make a fool of myself?" I questioned.

"You'll have the three of us to make sure you don't. Plus you are kind of part of Justin's plan to surprise her."

"Ok fine, but the moment I want out I can hide in one of the spare bedrooms, because I am assuming we will be spending the night, and no one is allowed to say no," I stated.

"Ok, ok," he said, holding his hands up in defense. We talked about random things for the rest of our run and then we talked in the backyard until dinner was ready. He told me about his friends and how they can't wait to graduate. He didn't necessarily say it, but I can tell that he feels a little sad, because he doesn't know what he wants to do after he graduates. After that we went in for dinner and we saw our mom, dad, and grandparents, my dad's parents, who had come to spend the night. It was my mom's turn to say grace.

"Dear Lord," she started. "Thank you for giving us the opportunity to gather as a family and enjoy this meal. Bless the hands that cooked this meal and bless the people who will eat it. We pray for those who are not as fortunate as us and hope they will be given what they need. Amen."

"Amen," we all repeated. The rest of the night was full of laughs and heartfelt stories about when dad was younger, because his mom felt like embarrassing him.

After we were done eating, Austin and I went up to his room and called Justin. Callie was at the movies with one of her friends, so we had hours to plan. We decided I would take her out to a restaurant while they got everything set up. By the time we got back, they would have everything set up and guests would have arrived. Now I just had to find the guts to go to a real party in one week.

Chapter 3
Party

After many secret phone calls and messages in between Austin, Justin, and me, we had finally planned the perfect party for Callie. I had to go pick her up for supper in about 20 minutes, but I had no idea what to wear. I am going to wear it to the party as well, but I have never been to a party before. I decided to wear my black leggings, my light blue tank top, and my white shoes. I did my hair half up and curled it. I wasn't too sure if it followed the whole party theme, but I felt comfortable in it so I was ok with that. I also had a bag packed since we were spending the night. Then I heard a knock at my door. It was Austin.

"Are you ready to go?"

"Ya I think so," I replied with a little bit of nervousness in my voice.

"C'mon, it will be fun!" he insisted. I grabbed my bag and Callie's gift, and then we left. Austin let me pick the music, so I put on my playlist. My playlist is a lot different than his, so when he lets me do this I have to play the music I like. He never complains, but I know that he doesn't like it. I am in the middle of screaming the words to a song when he decides to roll down the windows to let me yell even louder. Being with my brother has always been my safe space. He never judged me. I was thinking about this as I was screaming when I had a horrible memory.

It was last year when I was at school and waiting for everyone else to come for lunch. I hated being in the cafeteria alone, because it was so loud and crowded. I was looking at my phone trying to not bring attention to myself when Beth, the girl I thought was my friend until she turned on me about a year before this, sat down with her boyfriend.

"What are you doing?" she asked me.

"Probably looking at your Instagram, Beth," James, her boyfriend, replied to her. "She is kind of obsessed with you."

"What do you want, Beth?" I asked.

"Just checking in on you. Do you have any secrets you want to tell me?" she questioned me, laughing with James.

"Can you please just leave me alone?" I asked, trying to get out of the situation.

"I mean I could, but I don't really want to, " she said, and then her boyfriend dumped a bottle of pop on my head. Everyone around us laughed, and I was close to crying when Beth leaned in close to me. "I still haven't told anyone about your biggest insecurities. It felt too sad to tell. You know you should be thanking me for not telling anyone."

"Thanking you after what you did to her?" I heard Callie say from behind her. I didn't even realize that Austin and Justin were standing with her until they had ripped James out of his chair. Before I knew it Beth and Callie were yelling at each other, my brother was punching James in the face, and Justin was holding him back so he couldn't fight. All of this chaos happened, because I couldn't stand up for myself.

I was still lost in thought and I must have stopped singing, because when we pulled up to a stop light my brother was snapping his fingers in my face.

"You okay?" he asked.

"Yeah, yeah I'm just thinking," I replied, looking at him. He gave me a look that told me he knows I am lying but doesn't ask any more questions. There were about two more minutes of the drive, so we didn't talk much. When we pulled up to the house, he looked straight at me.

"Just so you know, unless someone broke the "don't invite other people" rule, Beth and James won't be at the party."

"Okay, thanks."

"No problem. Ok, let's make this party happen," he said, smiling at me. We stepped out of the car, and I grabbed my bag and Callie's present. Austin had his bag in hand and locked the car door as we walked to the entrance. Austin knocked on the door and Callie almost immediately answered the door.

"Happy birthday!" we both exclaimed, as I held up the present.

"Thank you so much you guys!" I handed her the present, and then Austin and I went to put our bags in two of the spare bedrooms. After that she opened the present to find the shirt that she has been wanting for almost 3 months. She started jumping up and down and running to show Justin, who was in the kitchen making supper for him and Austin. She told me that she wanted to wear it to dinner, so she ran to change and I called an Uber. Justin had made sure that I remembered he wanted us to be back by 8:30 and that I couldn't bring her home any earlier. When we left, they both waved goodbye from the window and then quickly moved along. I assumed it was because Justin was stressing out and wanted everything to be perfect, so he wanted to have as much time as possible.

When Callie and I got to the restaurant, I could tell she was excited. It was barely ever the two of us. I knew she missed it, because we used to do it all of the time. We talked about so much. She told me about her new crush which was fun to hear about. We talked about quite a bit, we ate, and I managed to stall her for about 2 hours. It was now 8 o'clock. By the time the Uber that I just called arrived and took us back, it would be 8:30. I paid for the food and then we stood outside. When the Uber driver picked us up, Callie was in the middle of telling me about her friend group drama and having a complete stranger in the front seat did not stop her one bit.

I had a sudden feeling of anxiety when we pulled up to the house, but I couldn't let Callie see that because she didn't even know this was happening. We walked to the door and when she opened it, she saw everyone who was invited standing there.

"Happy Birthday!!" everyone exclaimed.

Callie was really happy. First she hugged me, then Justin, and finally Austin. People around us got right into partying. Music was already playing and everyone was talking. I found it to be way too loud, but I tried to pretend to have fun. My aunty and uncle weren't there, but they did know the party was happening. My aunty and uncle are pretty chill. They just want their kids to be able to have fun, so it didn't surprise me when they approved the party. It felt like there were so many people there. All of Callie's friends and teammates were at the party, along with my brother and Justin's friend group, some people on my brother's team, plus people that kind of know Callie.

It seemed like everyone was dancing to the music as they talked to their friends. I thought that it would be fun if I were able to do that, but I just didn't know a lot of people. When I looked at my brother, I saw that he and Justin were having a lot of fun with a few of their friends. It was nice to see, because I have never seen them in this element. They both had some of the biggest smiles I have ever seen on their faces, and I knew that they were going to be going to a lot of parties this year. Then I looked at Callie, and I knew that the feeling of discomfort that I had was all worth it. These last few years of high school were going to be great for her.

I was starting to feel really uncomfortable with everyone around me, so I decided to go to the kitchen and get a pop from the cooler. I opened it to see a whole lot of beer, which I thought was odd because Callie didn't drink, but I guess it was a high school party. I dug to the bottom of the cooler to find a couple different kinds of pop and grabbed a can of this new kind of pop I thought I would try. I didn't love it, but I did finish it. People came and went in the kitchen, but nobody bothered me. My brother came in at about midnight to check on me, but I told him I was fine and that he should go back to the party side of everything. He hesitated, but he eventually decided that he would just leave me be.

Everyone who had been invited was gone by about two. Most people who had come either got Ubered there and back or friend groups had a designated driver, so there were only our vehicles left. I went into the spare bedroom I always stay in when I spend the night and changed into my pajamas. I sat on the bed for a bit looking around the room. There was a picture of the four of us and some pictures hung on the wall. There was a night stand, a dresser, and a desk all with lamps on them. The walls were painted a pale blue and Aunty decorated the room with throw pillows and a wooden chair in the corner. I turned off all of the lamps and looked at the pictures on the walls until I finally fell asleep.

Chapter 4
Weekend

Usually when Austin and I spend the night at Callie and Justin's house we get up super early. There is no reason behind it, but we always have. Aunty would make us pancakes and the cousins would put a bunch of different toppings in bowls. When our uncle finally got up, he would make fresh orange juice. It was always my favorite part of the day, because everyone was smiling. Sometimes my parents would even come over. It was always a lot of fun.

I knew my Aunty wasn't home, so I knew the pancakes were definitely not happening but for some reason I still got up at seven. I stayed in the spare bedroom for a while and went on my phone. I eventually got bored, so I changed into some clothes and went out into the living room to see the mess that was left from yesterday. I started to quietly clean up the cups, cans, and other garbage that was left sitting around. I started to think about last night and had this sudden feeling of regret. I realized that if I was willing to go out of my comfort zone maybe I would have been able to have fun like everyone else that was here. If I ever go to a party again maybe I will try and have a bit of fun. I suddenly saw pop spilled on the table which snapped me out of last night's regret, and it sent me back into the spiral of yesterday's remembering.

The fight got each member of my family suspended, but I didn't go to school until they were allowed. Our parents came to pick us up and the only problem was they had no idea I was being bullied. I had to explain it all to them, but they weren't mad at me, they were just upset that this happened. They weren't even really mad at my brother because without him the bullying would have been a lot worse. He did get the "fighting is not the answer" speech, and he did get his phone taken for a few days because he got suspended. I felt so terrible that my brother was getting in trouble because of me, and I was worried my cousins were too. I was still covered in pop on the drive home, and I was dreading trying to get all of it out of my hair. I looked at my brother to realize he was already looking at me. He gave me the smile he did when we were younger. It was the one he gave that reassured me he wasn't mad at me. I still felt like it was my fault though. Like if I could have stood up for myself, Beth and James wouldn't have done that to me, and my family wouldn't have had to step in.

I was sitting on the living room floor crying, reliving one of the worst days of my life. My knees were up close to my chest, arms crossed resting on my knees with my head down, sobbing. I didn't even realize when Austin walked in the room until he had sat down next to me and put his arm around me. I sobbed some more but this time with my head resting on his shoulder. He didn't ask any questions, probably because he knew I wouldn't be able to spit it out. We sat like this for about ten minutes until I had finally gained my composure, and he finally felt safe to ask a question.

"Is this related to whatever happened on the way here yesterday?" he asked quietly, being careful not to wake the other two. I slowly nodded my head.

"What is it?"

"Well there have been all these reminders recently," I began, "about the fight last year. I can't help but keep feeling like it's all my fault. Like if I could have stood up for myself this wouldn't have happened, and life would have been easier. Mom and Dad wouldn't know it even happened, and the three of you wouldn't have gotten in trouble. I mean what if universities hold it against you and getting into a good school gets harder for you? I would never be able to live with myself if I found out I was the reason that your future is going to be even harder than it already will be. I might have ruined everything for you guys and-"

"Hey, relax okay? We might have been standing up for you, but the decisions we made were entirely up to us. Callie chose to swear and yell at Beth, and Justin and I chose to fight James. You need to stop blaming yourself. None of us blame you for anything that happened that day, and none of us regret doing it either. We would do it again in a heartbeat if we needed to, okay?" he looked right at me. I nodded my head.

"He's right you know," I heard Callie say from the living room entrance. I look over to see her and Justin standing in the doorway.

"How long have you been there?" I asked them, a little worried.

"We heard almost all of it," Justin replied. "And you should know that I would a hundred and ten percent beat up James again." I smiled. I thought it was pretty funny considering he is not really one for violence.

"Thanks guys," I said.

"Okay let's go get some breakfast and then we can finish cleaning," Callie said.

We didn't want to make pancakes, because no one could make them like Aunty did. We decided that we would make bacon and eggs with hashbrowns and toast. It might have been a lot, but we all like to eat these things, and we love breakfast. Justin was making the bacon, Callie made the eggs, I made the hashbrowns, and my brother toasted the bread, buttered it and poured us the orange juice that was already made by my Uncle in the fridge. We sat down at the table, and we made plans to go to Austin's football game on Monday which would be fun. We also thought it would maybe be fun to go bowling either today or tomorrow. Once we finished breakfast we did the dishes and finished getting ready. We were then finally able to finish cleaning which was good.

We were sitting on the couch and watching TV, but I was too zoned out to even be paying attention. There was this one day a while ago that I have never told anyone about. I thought it was too embarrassing. I was sitting in Math when this girl I didn't know walked up to me.
"So you can't stand up for yourself and you got your family suspended?" she asked me harshly.

"What?"

"If you just stood up to Beth on your own, your family wouldn't have gotten in trouble. I'm sure they were really happy with you."

"Just leave me alone please," I sounded desperate to get out of there. I didn't care because I was.

"Okay fine then, but I just think it's pretty sad." Then she got up and walked out of the classroom. I realized that the bell hadn't even rung yet so it made sense that she wasn't part of this class and that I didn't know her.

That's something I never wanted to tell anyone, because I couldn't stand it if they found out. It shows that even though Beth picks on me the most, other people will do it sometimes too and I don't want them to feel like they have to protect me from everyone, because they don't. And they can't. It's impossible to do that, and it would be exhausting for them to even try. I was lost in my own thoughts when their conversation finally caught my attention.

"You guys should spend another night," Callie said.

"Yes! Our parents aren't even home until tomorrow, and I'm sure they would love to see you guys," Justin joined in.

"Yeah sure, why not," I said.

"Okay. I'll call our parents to let them know what the plan is," my brother said, as he took out his phone and walked away.

"Just so you know," Justin started, "I don't want you to feel bad about what happened. None of us do. Plus we were in grade 10 and grade 9. The chances of universities holding us to one suspension is slim to none, especially in those grades," he explained, and Callie had a soft smile on her face.

"Thanks," I said looking at the two of them.

"Anytime," Justin said. We sat in awkward silence for a minute.

"We should order pizza for lunch!" Callie exclaimed, breaking the silence and changing the subject.

"One hundred percent!" I loudly said.

"Yeah for sure," Justin confirmed.

"Did I hear you guys planning on ordering pizza?" Austin asked as he walked around the hallway corner and into the living room.

"Yeah!" Callie replied.

"Thank goodness. I'm so hungry!"

When we ordered the pizza, we decided that it would be fun to do what we always do… build a fort. It may seem dumb that teenagers our age are building a fort on the living room floor but for us it wasn't. Even when the parents were home, or at Christmas time, we always built a fort. We did it at Christmas time, because it was fun to watch movies in it. We did it whenever we ordered pizza, because it has been a tradition since we were 6 and 7. Austin and Justin moved all of the furniture to the outsides of the living room while Callie and I went to get the blankets and pillows from the rooms the four of us use. We used an extra long sheet that was able to cover the entire middle of the living room that we pinned to two tall kitchen chairs. Then we found four sheets to drape on each side of the fort. We used the two heaviest blankets on the bottom and put the pillows along the back of the fort. Then we put the rest of the blankets in just in case someone got cold. We also got the old lantern that we always used to turn on if we wanted to watch a movie. By the time the fort was built the pizza had come and there were four teenagers sitting in a fort eating pizza in the middle of the living room. Just like they did when they were 6 and 7. In that moment, I let myself forget about all of the bad in my life and just be happy with my family.

We all fell asleep on the couches and floors of the living room. When we finally got up the next morning, we decided that we should probably clean up before my Aunty and Uncle got home. It actually didn't take that long to clean up. When they got back, they were surprised but happy to see that Austin and I were there. They suggested that our parents come over for supper and before I knew it the plans were set. We thought it would be best to go bowling before supper, so we booked a lane for two o'clock. It gave us about an hour to eat lunch and get ourselves organized.

When we got to the bowling alley, we realized that booking a lane was the right decision. There had to have been three birthday parties and at least two sports teams doing team building. We got our shoes and got organized.

"Hey, we should go and pick a song!" Callie said to me. "Do you have a dollar?"

"Yeah I think so."

"Great, let's go!" She grabbed my hand and ran to the music. The bowling alley we go to is themed by different decades. The diner is set in the 1950's where you find the jukebox. It isn't exactly like a jukebox in the sense that it is connected to every speaker and there isn't a limit of songs, but it is shaped like a jukebox and you have to pay a dollar. Callie decided on a song that I didn't know but she clearly enjoyed. We went to our lane and Austin and Justin brought back some donuts and pop.

"Okay I think we are ready," my brother said after taking a sip of his pop. Like the 1960s, the actual bowling section had benches that alternated color between orange and white. They are definitely more comfortable than they would have been in the 60s, but it still matched the theme. When it was my turn, I went up and grabbed a green ball. I quickly realized after the ball left my hands that I am not a super strong bowler, but I am definitely not the worst. After my three tries I only had two pins left so that was pretty good. Austin got a strike and surprised no one, Callie did about the same as me, and Justin did pretty bad. The rest of the game kind of went at a similar pace with Austin winning, Callie coming in second, I came in third, and Justin came last. He did get better as the game went on though.

"We should go to the arcade," Justin said.

"Why? Because you're better at that?" Callie asked.

"Well, yeah!" he said.

"Ok fine, because you stuck with it and played the entire bowling match, we can go to the arcade with you," Austin said. I just nodded my head. I didn't really care what we did next as long as we did something.

When you walk into the arcade the first thing that catches your eye is all the brightly colored shapes on the carpet. The second thing is all of the colored lights.It really shows the 80s in one room. We spent a very long time in the arcade until everyone but Justin got extremely tired of it.

"Come on Justin, we want to go home!" Callie said right to his face.

"Just let me have one more round!" He said, eyes locked on the screen.

"Fine!" My brother sounded a little annoyed, but that was just him trying to get out of there.

"We are going to grab milkshakes, so if you want to stay and play your game you can, but we are not staying here," I said.

"Wait, milkshakes! No one said anything about milkshakes!" he said, finally looking at the three of us.

"You're such a four year old!" stated Callie as we began walking to the food.

Once we got our milkshakes, we decided to go home so we were there when my parents got there. When we did get home our efforts to make it home before my mom and dad had failed, but they didn't seem to mind.

"Hey guys!" My aunty started, "dinner is going to be ready in 20 minutes."

We sat down and mostly just listened to the parents talk. Every odd time I would look at one of the other three when a parent said something weird, and we did our best not to laugh. When we ate supper we were allowed to talk a little bit, but I still didn't say much. It was a pretty good meal. We did have to leave earlier than usual though, because it was a school night. My parents rode in their car, and I rode with Austin. All in all, it was a pretty good weekend.

Chapter 5
Football

"C'mon Nicole, we are going to be late for school!" my brother yelled, as he banged on my door.

"Just give me a second!" I really was almost ready. I just needed to put my binder in my backpack. Once I was done, I swung my door open. Austin was still standing there.

"You ready?" he questioned.

"Yep," I said, as we made our way down the stairs. We put our shoes on and walked out the door. On the drive he didn't say much, which was not like him, so I asked him about it.

"Hey, are you ok? You're kind of quiet."

"Ya, I'm just thinking."

"About what?" I knew he wasn't telling me something, and I couldn't let it be.

"You know my football game today?"

"Yeah."

"Okay, well apparently some people from a couple different universities are coming. It is not very likely for them to sign an eleventh grader, but the coach said if I impress them then they might offer me a conditional scholarship. Then what they would do is come and watch a couple of my games in grade twelve to see if I am still worth a scholarship."

"Isn't that a good thing? You only ever used to talk about getting a football scholarship!"

"Yeah, but now it's here, and it's scary. I mean I've been thinking about it a lot, and I don't know if I want to play football after high school anymore."

"Wait, why not?"

"Well it's hard to be an athlete in high school. I can only imagine what it is like when you are at college or university."

"Where are the scouts from?"

"Some colleges. Mostly universities though." I could tell he wanted to say something else, but he stopped himself.

"What else is it?" I know that it is more than just difficulty. He loves a challenge.

"Playing for a university football team," he paused, "It was always dad's dream. Don't get me wrong, I love football, but I don't know if I love it enough to go that far with it. If I don't, then dad will be so upset that neither of us fulfilled his dream."

"Can I offer a suggestion?" I asked.

"Depends what it is," he replied, pulling up to a stop light.

"Play the game as hard as you can. Don't finish the game with any ounce of energy in you. If they don't sign you, I guess you can consider that fate making a decision for you. Because you are not in grade 12, they are not going to make you commit until next season. They will show interest in you though and will probably let you know that they are coming back next year. That means you have a whole year to decide what you want to do. Okay?"

"Yeah, okay," he replied. The rest of the ride was thankfully like normal. He was finally being talkative the rest of the drive.

Once we got to school, I wasn't surprised to see Callie and Justin already standing by Austin's locker. I don't know why, but that has always been our meeting point every year. It doesn't matter what floor his locker was on, it was always his. It is probably because the most likely to be driving the four of us at the same time is Austin.

"Hey guys!" Callie exclaimed, waving her hand.

"Hey! How's it going?" I asked.

"Not bad," they both said at the same time. We talked for a bit until we all had to go to our first class of the day. When I got to mine, I immediately noticed who was sitting in the front row today. Beth. The way she looked at me felt as though her brown eyes were shooting daggers at me.

"Hey, Nicole," she said in her usual mean voice.

"Hi, Beth," I replied, as I walked to the back corner of the classroom. To my surprise, she didn't follow or taunt me. I sat down at the corner desk. I don't know why I like to sit here so much but I do. There is a window on my left with a couple little plants, and I am not surrounded by a bunch of people. I can also see the board pretty well. This is the best part of my school day: the calm before class starts.

The rest of the day was pretty much the same as it always is. Beth had a few comments about my outfit that she didn't fail to mention, but I tried not to let it bother me. Besides, I needed to focus on my brother. It's a big day. I headed to the football field and walked over to the bleachers to see our school team warming up. Justin and Callie were already sitting down.

"Hey! How do you think they are going to do?" I asked them.

"Well their warm up is going pretty good, but so did the other team's. It looks like it is going to be a really close game," Justin replied to me, as he observed what was left of the warmup.

"Does anyone else think Austin looks nervous?" Callie asked. "He is not playing like it, but it kind of looks like he is."

"Yeah well," I hesitated. I don't know if Austin wants them to know or not, but I feel like they deserve to know because the three of us are his biggest supporters, besides dad. "People from colleges and universities are here today. He's nervous because he needs to stand out for them to show interest in signing him next year."

"Oh wow," Callie replied.

"It's a big game then," Justin started. "Do your parents know?"

"No, not yet," I replied. He never told me this, but I had this feeling that it was because he didn't want them to feel bad. Because of their jobs, they can't make it to very many of his games.

"Well I hope he does well," Justin said.

"Yeah me too," I said as I looked out at the field. The game was about to start.

Austin played the best game I have ever seen him play. His team won, but it was a super close game. The three of us went to go talk to him, but it looked like we were beaten to it. There was a line of maybe four men in different university gear. It took him a while, but he was finally free and ready to go home. He came over to the three of us smiling.

"Did you guys see that?" he asked excitedly. "There are four different university teams interested in signing me next year!"

"That's great!" I said.

"Congrats!" Callie exclaimed.

"That's awesome Austin," Justin stated.

"I'm tired, so I should probably go home, but thanks guys so much for coming," Austin said, patting Justin on the back of his shoulder.

"Of course! See you later," Callie replied.

"Yeah, bye guys," Justin said.

"See you later," I said as I waved. Austin and I turned and started walking towards the car.

"So, are you reconsidering what you said this morning?" I asked him.

"I think so. I know it was dad's dream, but I think I could have a lot of fun doing it. The way they were talking, we would barely have to pay any money. I'm just not sure I can be committed to a university team and that is my biggest worry."

"Well, you don't have to decide today," I told him.

"Yeah, you're right. Can you do me a favor and not tell our parents for a little while."

"Of course, but you have to tell them eventually."

"I know, but I want to be closer to a decision before I tell them," he said as he started the car. I never thought my brother would be this way with decisions. He usually knows exactly what he wants right away. He never even had to take a day to think about what classes he wanted to take. I guess I kind of get it though. A sports team is a huge commitment, let alone a university team. I guess he will have to decide on his own.

Chapter 6
Thanksgiving

I don't know why, but Thanksgiving has always been a big deal in our family. I don't know if it is because of how much they like the dinner, how much my mom and Aunty love expressing gratitude, or if it is just because it's an excuse for our family to get together, but it is a huge deal. We are all expected to dress semi-nice, which I don't mind. It's kind of nice to see everyone in a nice outfit, because it only ever happens on Thanksgiving and Christmas day.

I was in my room getting ready, and it took me a minute to decide what to wear. I decided on a long sleeve burgundy top with my jeans and white shoes. I pulled my hair back into a braid and put on a little mascara and blush. I walked out of my room to see my brother standing in the hallway. He had a blue and white plaid shirt and a pair of jeans. He had the same old pair of shoes he always has on, but I think those are the only ones that he feels comfortable wearing.

"You look half way too nicely dressed for once," he said to me.

"Jee thanks." I replied. "Where are mom and dad?"

"They already left," he answered. "They said something about wanting to help Grandma set up. Are you ready to go?"

"Yep!" I said jumping. He laughed at me, but I was okay with that. I basically ran down the stairs, excited to get to Grandma and Grandpa's. Austin came quickly after me, probably because he knew how impatient I would get. I hopped in the passenger seat and waited for him to get in and start the car.

"Can you turn on my playlist?" he asked me when he got in.

"Yeah for sure," I said. An older song came on as soon as I put it on. He loved old music. Smiling, he started drumming on the steering wheel and singing along. I laughed at him. I know this is probably how he feels when I'm screaming songs in the passenger seat of his car, but it doesn't bother me. I looked out the window to see what was happening in town today. There wasn't anything exciting, but one of the older restaurants had a trivia night for Thanksgiving.

"Looks like our parents are the only ones that are here yet," Austin said as he pulled up to our grandparent's house.

"That's okay," I said, "I like visiting with our grandparents."

"I know, because Grandma always tells you about high school, and Grandpa always tells you about his family," he stated matter of factly.

"Oh whatever! Grandpa always talks to you about sports and you love it," I replied.

"Yeah that's true," he said as he stopped the car engine. We both stepped out of the car and walked up the stairs to the front door. Austin's hand went up to knock on the door.

"Hey," I said, "remember what Grandma says every time you knock on the door?"

"I know, but it just feels wrong not to," he said.

"Okay go ahead then," I said. He knocked on the door. About thirty seconds later, Grandma came to the door.

"Austin! Nicole! Come in!" She said ushering us in. "Now, how many times do I have to tell you to just let yourself in? Everyone else in the family does it!"

"I know Grandma," Austin said. "Maybe next time."

"It looks amazing here, Grandma," I said.

"Well thank you, but your mom helped me a lot. She actually did most of it," Grandma replied. I looked around. The table had the fall leaves tablecloth and fancy china. There were a couple pumpkin decorations in the living room along with a couple of acorn decorations around them. The rest of the decorations were the same: the globe on the side table in the living room, the family photos, and then the four school photos of the four grandchildren. I saw my dad getting the cutter out, so when it was time, my grandpa could cut the turkey. It wasn't anywhere near being time, but my dad liked to help out, and he liked to be prepared. I saw my mom looking at a photo of her and her sister when they were younger, but she looked kind of sad. I decided to go over to her.

"Are you okay?" I asked, as I walked over to her.

"Yeah I'm okay. I just remembered something," she replied.

"Mind me asking what?"

"Just about the old treehouse."

"You guys had a treehouse?" I was surprised.

"Yeah we did, but it got too old for it to be safe and your grandpa had to take it down."

"Oh."

"Yeah, but that's okay. By the time they took it down, we were too big to do anything but sit in it anyways," she said. She looked better already. I think it is probably because she had just thought about it and wanted to talk about the nostalgia.

"I am gonna go help get dinner ready," she said smiling.

"Okay," I replied. I stood there for a moment, looking at the picture. My mom and aunty looked really similar, especially when they were younger. Then I decided to walk over to my brother. He was sitting on the couch in the living room flipping through the pages of the newest book my grandpa was reading and must have left out.

"Do you want to go downstairs with me?" I asked him.

"Sure," he answered. We walked to the staircase and then down the stairs. We turned around the wall that separated the stairs and the hallway and then walked down the short hallway. In the middle of the basement living room there was a wooden table with four barstool chairs where people play card games. It wasn't really the same theme as the rest, but it came from my grandpa's family, so I guess it made sense that they would want to keep it. There were a lot of pictures on the walls of my grandparents when they were younger, my mom and aunty, and the grandchildren. My brother plopped himself on the couch.

"So what did you even want to do down here?" he questioned me.

"Give me one second," I answered, moving quickly down the hallway. I turned into the spare bedroom and opened the closet. My grandma kept all the photo books down here except for the ones she wanted to display upstairs. I studied the shelves until I found the one I was looking for. I grabbed it and went back out into the living room.

"How many times can you look at photos from our first family Christmas trip?" he asked me.

"I love these photos," I responded.

"I know you do," He told me.

"Scooch over," I told him, and he did. We looked through all of the photos together, laughing at what we looked like when we were 5 and 4. There was this one picture at the end of the book of the four of us on the beach in Hawaii, and it will always be my favorite in the book. Once we had finished, I went to put it back and grab a different book. When I set the book on the shelf, I heard the door open and people saying hello.

"They're here!" I yelled down the hallway to my brother.

"I'm coming!" he yelled back at me. I waited for him to walk to where I was and then we made our way up the stairs.

"Hey guys!" Callie said as we walked to the door.

"Hey!" I said back and gave her a hug.

"Oh c'mon. You guys literally saw each other at school two days ago!" Justin said.

"Well I can still give her a hug," I told him.

"Hey Nicole, can I borrow you for a second?" I heard my grandpa ask from the kitchen.

"Yeah for sure!" I replied. "I'll be back in a minute," I said to the three of them as I walked over to my grandpa. I noticed on my way that my uncle and aunty were already busy helping in the kitchen.

"Come with me," my grandpa said. I followed him down the stairs and into his office. He used to work from home a lot when my mom and her sister were little and ever since he kept his office.

"I want to show you something," he told me, as he walked over to his shelf. He pulled out one of the books he keeps of family history. They have so many pictures, documents, and stories, and I have always found them interesting.

"I was going through this book yesterday, and I found something I thought you might want to read," he said to me. He pulled out a paper and handed it to me. On the top it was labeled *Anderson*, my mom's maiden name.

"You probably know that Anderson has been a family name for a while because of all the history documents you have read about it," my grandpa said. "But I thought you would want to know where it came from and maybe have a family tree to keep it in order."

"Thanks Grandpa," I said, giving him a hug. I really do like reading things like this. It's really important to me.

"Of course," he said. "I'm going to help finish dinner. When you're done, you can just leave the paper on the desk." I nodded my head and then he started walking up the stairs. I got right to reading and learned a lot. The history part was mostly about my great- great- great- grandparents. It was pretty far back, but it was still interesting. The family tree was huge but cool to look at. I set the paper on the desk and walked out of the office. I heard my brother's voice in the basement living room, and I assumed he was talking to Callie and Justin. I walked down to the end of the hallway and sure enough the three of them were sitting at the wooden table. I walked to the last chair in between my brother and Callie.

"Learn anything?" My brother asked me.

"Everytime I come here I learn something," I replied.

"Fair enough," he said.

"We should probably go upstairs. Grandpa has been done cutting turkey for 5 minutes," Callie told me.

"Okay sounds good," I said. We all made our way upstairs and saw the adults sitting at the table waiting. We prayed and then got straight to eating. It was a great night with my family. We don't all get together at the grandparents very often. When we do, it is pretty special, and today was one of those days.

Chapter 7
Fun

"Please come with me tonight," Callie pleaded as I put my books in my locker and grabbed my backpack.

"Callie, I won't know anyone but you," I told her.

"Yes, you will. The party is only for grade ten. You will know almost everyone there," she argued.

"Yeah, but I won't really know them. In case you haven't noticed, I'm not a social butterfly," I countered.

"C'mon just once come with me. Maybe you will like it," she said desperately.

"Why do you want me to come? I won't have any fun if I do," I asked.

"Because I want you to get out of your comfort zone for a night and maybe have some fun," she said. I thought about it. I guess it wouldn't be the worst thing to just try and go to a party again. I did say I would try and have more fun if I ever went to another one. Plus, I could always get my brother to come pick me up if I needed.

"Okay fine. One party," I decided.

"Great!" she exclaimed.

"Okay, I have to go before Austin leaves without me," I said slowly starting to walk away. She followed me.

"I will be at your house at 7 to get ready, and then we can leave at 8:30," she stated as we walked out the doors and to the student parking lot. "Can you see if your brother will drive us?" she asked me.

"Sure," I said.

"Okay bye!" she said as she got into Justin's car.

"Bye," I replied. I walked to Austin's car, and he was talking to some of his friends. I didn't remember their names, but I never really needed to. It sounded like they were talking about football, so I just sat in the passenger seat and waited until they were done. I heard him say goodbye soon after and then he got into the driver's seat.

"Hey, how's it going?" he asked as he started the engine.

"Good," I replied. "I kind of have a favor to ask."

"Yeah what's up?" he questioned.

"So Callie kind of convinced me to go to this grade ten party. Could you maybe drive us?" I asked.

"Really? Wow, I can't believe she actually convinced you, and yeah I can drive you. I'll message Justin and see what he's up to."

"Okay, and if I need you to come and pick me up, you will?" I questioned him, worried.

"Yeah of course I can," he reassured me. The rest of the drive home I was silent, and he was singing to old songs. I was too busy thinking about the party to even think about laughing at him. I think he noticed how nervous I was because of the way he looked at me. It was the same look he gave me when I was nine, and he was ten. We were at the lake, and he forced me to try knee boarding for the first time. I was terrified. I didn't even really like tubing when we were going too fast. The look he gave me then was knowing I would have fun but feeling bad for pressuring me to do it. He was giving me the same look now. Knowing it would be good for me to get out of my comfort zone, but feeling bad, because he knows I'm terrified and don't want to.

Callie and Justin showed up at seven just like she said she would. She hurried me right up to my room.

"I think we should curl your hair, what do you think?" she asked once we got up to my room.

"Yeah sure," I responded. Hers was already curled and her makeup was done. I guess when she said get ready she meant help me get ready.

"What do you think you are going to do for makeup?" she questioned.

"I don't know. Nothing extreme," I answered.

"Okay, you do it while I do your hair," she said. Once she was done doing my hair and I finished my makeup, she went to our bathroom to get changed. I stood looking at my closet for about five minutes. I decided on a pale pink shirt and jeans with my white shoes. Once I had changed, I walked out into the hallway to see Callie already ready. She was wearing a tight black tank top and jeans with a pair of white shoes I have never seen her wear before. It was weird that our outfits matched, but it was kind of nice at the same time.

"Are you ready to go?" she asked me.

"I guess so," I responded nervously. We walked down the stairs to see Austin and Justin watching TV.

"Hey, can we leave?" Callie asked them.

"Yep!" my brother said. We all walked out the door and got into the car. I opened the door to the back seat thinking Justin would want to sit in the front, but my hands were shaking as I opened the door.

"Hey Nicole, why don't you sit in the front?" I heard Justin say from behind me. I think he knew that I was nervous and would feel a little more comfortable if I sat where I usually do.

"Y-yeah sure thanks," I said, giving him a soft smile. I opened the passenger door and sat down next to my brother. He started the car, pulled out of the driveway, and started to drive to one of our classmate's house.

"Hey Austin, have you thought about football anymore?" Justin questioned.

"I mean, I guess I've been thinking about it a little bit," Austin replied.

"Do you know what you want to do?" Callie asked.

"No, not yet. I'm still trying to figure out how to tell my parents," he told us.

"That's okay. You don't have to know right away," I told him.

"Thanks," he said to me. For the rest of the drive, Callie told us about these two girls in her friend group that apparently didn't like her anymore.

"I'm not sad about it, because we didn't talk that much to begin with," she said "We never even really got to know each other and the only reason we were in the same friend group is the two girls play on one of my best friend's basketball team. Anyway the two girls aren't really hanging out with my friend group anymore."

"Why don't they like you?" I questioned.

"Well they came up to me and told me that they don't like how I am the one that usually leads the conversation, but when I asked them if they wanted to try and lead a conversation, they shook their heads. I proceeded to tell them that I don't want to lead the conversation all of the time, but no one else ever does, so what am I supposed to do?" she replied.

"Huh," Justin said, as my brother pulled up next to our classmate's house.

"Okay, bye guys!" Callie said excitedly, as she hopped out of the car. Justin got out of the back so when I left he could have the passenger seat, but he noticed I was having a hard time leaving. He and Callie went a little ways away from the car and talked while they waited. For the next five minutes me and my brother sat in silence as I tried to get myself out of the car but stopped each time I got close.

"You know you don't have to go," my brother started, "but I can come and pick you up ten minutes after I leave if you need me to. Plus you'll have Callie. She's always there when you need her, okay?"

"Yeah y-you're right," I said shakily. "Okay I'm gonna go, bye."

"See you later," he said to me. Once I got out of the car, I said goodbye to Justin and then Callie and I went inside the house. It was already packed with grade ten students, and it instantly overwhelmed me. My hands started to shake quicker than they normally do. My heart was beating quickly, but I told myself I would try and have fun. I did my best to try and keep it under control and walked further into the crowded house.

"Hey, will you be okay if I go and say hi to some people?" Callie asked me.

"Yeah for sure," I told her.

"Okay, come get me if you need me," she said as she left. The next 10 minutes were full of me trying to figure out how to have fun at this party. I walked over to this guy from my Math class and talked to him for a bit. He sits next to me in class, and he is on my brother's team, so we talk sometimes. Our conversation was short lived though, because he had all of his friends there. Other than him I really didn't know anyone, so I decided to go to the backyard. There were a couple groups of friends out there, but it was pretty peaceful on the deck which was what I needed.

"Fitting that you're out here," Beth's voice said from behind me, breaking the peace. Great. Just who I needed to hear from. "What are you doing here anyways?" she asked me.

"Why does it matter to you?" I questioned.

"Oh it doesn't. This just doesn't seem like your scene. I guess that's why you're sitting out here alone. When your brother's not here, you're even more lonely," she stated.

"Can I leave now?" I asked, standing up.

"Yeah, you might as well. I mean it's not like you have any friends here, or at all, and your cousin doesn't count. Not to mention you don't really have a personality that makes others want to get to know you, so this party is kind of a bust for you," she rudely remarked. I knew she was just trying to get a reaction out of me, and I wasn't going to let that happen.

"Great talk Beth, but I have to go," I said, holding back tears as I walked back in the house. I went straight for Callie. I saw her talking to one of her friends.

"Hey, can I talk to you for a minute?" I asked desperately.

"Yeah for sure," she told me. "Hey I'll talk to you later," she told her friend. I lead her right out the front door and to the sidewalk where no cars were parked.

"Hey what's going on?" she questioned.

"Beth came up to me and told me a bunch of jerk stuff about my personality, how I am super lonely, and I couldn't take in anymore." I was crying, I couldn't handle it.

"Hey it's alright," she said, hugging me. "Let's go home okay."

"No, you don't have to. I can just message my brother and then you can get a ride with your brother after," I told her.

"No, we can all go and watch a movie or something, okay?" she reassured me. I nodded my head.

"Can we not tell them why though?" I asked.

"I mean sure, but what are you going to tell them?" she asked me.

"I'll just say I wasn't feeling the greatest," I responded. Then I messaged my brother and said: *Hey, I'm not feeling the greatest. Stomach hurts a bit. Can you come pick us up?*

A couple minutes later he responded with a *Yeah, for sure.* We waited outside, and I made sure that it didn't look like I was crying. Once they pulled up, we both got into the back seat.

"Hey, everything okay?" My brother immediately asked.

"Yeah, just a little stomach ache," I told him, as I put my seatbelt on and used it as a way not to make eye contact. It's always easier for him to tell if I am lying when he can see the guilt of lying on my face. We drove home, but I am not too sure what they were talking about. I was in my head about what Beth had said to me. Once we got home though I tried to shake it off. We decided that we would watch a movie, but as soon as it was done, Callie and Justin left, and I went to bed.

"Goodnight," My brother said from outside of my room.

"Night."

Chapter 8
Truth

I really wasn't feeling myself after that party. I was in my room, and I hadn't left it since I got up this morning. I'm getting hungry, but I am scared to run into my brother. He always knew how to get the truth out of me, and I didn't want him to worry. Once when I had first told him about Beth when she was just starting to be terrible to me, he got super over protective. He was always worried about me, and I didn't want to put him through all of that ever again. I didn't know what to do with myself though. When I heard him leave, I rushed downstairs and quickly ate a bowl of cereal then quickly rushed up to the bathroom to get ready and went straight back into my room. I knew my brother had gone to the gym and would be back in about thirty minutes, but I would rather be safe than sorry. Once I was in my room, I replayed my conversation with Beth from last night and before I knew it I was crying, and then bawling. Maybe she was right. Maybe I am just too unlikeable to have friends other than my family. There is a good chance that I am too annoying or too emotional, or maybe I am just a bad friend. All these thoughts were racing through my head, and I couldn't handle them anymore. I just sat in the silence of my room and cried. The only sound in my room was the sound of my phone suddenly buzzing. Callie messaged me:
Hey, just checking in. You okay?

Still crying, I figured it would be better to just lie:
Yeah, I'm alright.

Seconds later she was responding:
Are you sure?

She knows me pretty well, but I didn't want her to worry:
Ya absolutely! :)

I put my phone down and rolled over to look at the picture on my nightstand. It was a picture of the four of us. It was the last trip we had gone on. We were in Hawaii like every Christmas Break and had spent the whole day at the beach. It was the hottest day of the trip, but we were all happy. We played beach volleyball for hours, went swimming, and ate a bunch of food. We took the picture at the end of the day and even though we were sweating to new extremes, we were smiling. The picture was of the four of us laughing as we made our way into the ocean. My mom took it. She knew I liked pictures like that, and she saw the perfect opportunity. Looking at that picture and remembering that day was enough to make me stop crying.

I was watching TV in my room when my brother got home. I half expected him to assume I had gone out with Callie, and I was okay with that. I heard him walk up the stairs and then I heard a knock at my door.

"Can I come in?" he asked.

"Yeah," I replied. He walked in the door and sat at the edge of my bed. I paused the TV so it wasn't playing in the background.

"So how was the party before you got sick?" he questioned.

"It was fine I guess," I lied.

"After I worked out I went over to Justin and Callie's," he informed me.

"She told you?" I asked.

"Well you hadn't come out of your room since last night which isn't like you, and I was worried so I asked her if something happened at the party. She tried to cover for you at first but then when I told her that you were hiding she got worried and told me about Beth," he told me. I started to tear up. The last thing I wanted was for people to worry about me, and I'm sure Justin is now too, so everyone is.

"Yeah well Beth told me that I was even sadder and more lonely when you aren't there and that cousins don't count as a good friend which in my mind is stupid, because they are our friends and then she told me that my personality isn't one that makes people want to be friends with me," I told him in an almost panic while shedding a few tears.

"Did it get to you?" he questioned. I nodded. "I know it's hard, but you should really try not to let it get to you. I don't know what happened to her, but she is clearly just trying to make your life miserable for no reason, and cousins do count as friends. Especially when it comes to our family. We are really close, and we choose to hang out together, and we choose to get together almost every weekend. I have quite a few friends, but none of them ever top the four of us. Plus look at it this way...I'm your brother. If you had an annoying personality, I wouldn't be hanging out with you."

"Whatever!" I said punching him in the arm. I don't know how he did it, but he made me stop crying, and he even made me smile a bit.

"Want to have a movie day in the basement?" he asked. "Mom and Dad aren't home all day. They went out with some friends or something. We could go buy junk food and order a pizza?"

"We watched a movie yesterday. Do you want to go out for lunch? I can pay," I suggested.

"We can go out for lunch in thirty minutes, but you're not paying," he said. After arguing about who was going to pay, Austin won. We went out for lunch, and it was fun. We went to this new fast food restaurant that just got into town, and it had some weird menu items, but the food we got was good. After we were done eating, we went home and had a relaxing rest of the day.

Chapter 9
Hawaii

It was finally my favorite time of year, our family Christmas trip to Hawaii. We always rent the same oceanfront condo in Wailea, Maui. My grandparents, Aunty and Uncle, and my parents all pitch in to pay for it, but my grandparents pay more than the others. We tend to eat on the cheaper side so we can afford the rental and flights. Each teen saves up and pays for one of the meals on the trip. We don't really do a lot of shopping, only a little. Instead, we spend every moment we can at the beach. Christmas was yesterday, and we spent it with my dad's family. I got money for the trip which is good. We leave tomorrow, and I am super excited.

We got up at two in the morning for an early flight. We left the house at three and got to the airport at about four. Once we met up with the rest of our family, we got through security and all of that, and then I took a nap until our plane arrived at 6:30am. Once we got on the plane, I sat next to my brother and my dad. I took another nap, because I was really tired and then my brother and I watched a few movies. We also ate quite a bit of food that Austin bought for us at the airport convenience store.

"Hey, are you excited?" he asked me.

"Oh c'mon. Do you even have to ask?" I responded.

"No, but I do every year," he pointed out.

"Fair enough," I told him.

"We should totally go to the beach as soon as we get there," he said.

"Of course we will! What else would we do?" I asked.

"I don't know" he shrugged. Eat food?"

"I think we've eaten enough food and bags of candy to last us until tomorrow without getting hungry," I told him.

"Yeah, you're probably right about that," he agreed. Then we heard the captain say that we were going to land right away, and I was smiling from ear to ear. When we landed, I could sense that my brother got a little tense. He was never the biggest fan of landing.

"You okay?" I asked.

"Yeah, I'll be fine," he replied.

Once we got off the airplane and got out of the airport, we called a car to pick us up and take us to our condo. I couldn't wait to get to my room. The people who rent it out always keep it the same. It has light blue walls and vases full of seashells. The bedspread is white and so is the dresser and the desk. There was a lamp on the nightstand and a few pictures of the beach. It also had a huge window where you could see the ocean. Everytime we come, we have the same bedrooms. I don't know why, but we do. The car pulled up to the house, and I hopped out of the car, grabbed my bags, and ran straight for the door.

"Hey wait for us!" I heard Callie yell.

"Yeah, how are you going to get in without a key?" I heard my grandma ask. I just shrugged my shoulders. I was just happy to be here. Austin, Callie, and Justin came up to the door and waited with me for grandma to come and unlock the door.

"As soon as we get in, we should change into bathing suits and go. No wasting time," I said.

"Of course!" Callie exclaimed. "I have been waiting to go for a swim all week!" Austin and Justin laughed and nodded their heads. My grandma came and unlocked the door.

"First one in the water wins!" My brother hollered as he ran up the stairs. We all quickly ran up the stairs behind him. I bolted into my room and ripped open my suitcase. I quickly changed into the first bathing suit I could find and rushed out of the house. I didn't think to bring a towel, because we would be in the sun for a while after so I wouldn't really need to dry off. My brother was only a couple of feet ahead of me and Justin was on my tail with Callie close behind. We all ran into the water and even though my brother got there first, we were all pretty close.

"I win!" My brother said, "Just like last summer and the summer before that."

"Oh whatever!" Callie said, annoyed with him.

"What? It's true!" he told her. I decided to splash him, so I flung a ton of water at him.

"Hey!" he shouted and then flung even more water at me. Before I knew it, Callie and Justin were joining in, and we were in this huge water fight. It was a lot of fun and really funny to watch someone's reaction when someone splashed them out of nowhere. We spent almost the entire day in the water (except for when we got hungry, and we needed to eat). Then I went to bed and fell asleep almost instantly.

The next day I got up at about 6: 30 and ate a bowl of cereal on the porch. All of the adults went out to buy some groceries for the week, and I just got lucky with finding where they put our cereal. I didn't think anyone was going to be up for a while, but I was ok with that. I liked being alone out here early in the morning. You could smell the ocean and there was a breeze, but it was still warm out. The best part about it was it was detached from the rest of my life. Beth wasn't here to bother me, school wasn't here, and no one was making fun of me for not being extremely social or anything like that. It was just me and my family at the beach and that is all I need to be happy.

My brother came out at about eight thirty with a bowl of cereal. He sat down next to me and looked out at the ocean.

"Morning," he said.

"Morning," I replied.

"Do you want to go for an early morning swim?" he questioned.

"Yeah sure. I will go get ready," I replied. I went to the bathroom to brush my teeth, wash my face, and brush my hair. Then I went to change into my bathing suit. On the way out, I ran into my brother who had already changed. He must have eaten his breakfast really quickly. We grabbed towels and went to the ocean. We spent about an hour in the water until everyone else was up and ready.

"Hey, you guys want to play some volleyball?" Callie called from shore.

"Yeah, for sure!" my brother yelled back. We all helped set up the net that the renters let us use, and because it was early, there was no one around that would be bothered by us.

"Okay boys vs girls?" Callie asked.

"Yep," Justin said. We played three sets, and the girls won.

"Yes!" Callie yelled when we got the last point.

"There's no way! You guys have never won a volleyball game before!" Justin exclaimed.

"Yeah right!" I said to him. We decided that we should move the net onto the grass of the condo's property. It was a pretty decent distance, but we made it. The rest of the day we spent outside, just the four of us. The adults went to look around town and probably to get a break from how annoying the four of us could be on these trips. We spent the day in the water, on the beach, and in the yard. It was great.

The week went by super fast and before I knew it I was packing up my bag. I hate leaving this place. My favorite place on earth. The only peaceful place that makes me a hundred percent happy all of the time, and I have to leave. Everytime we come I wish the same thing: that we had enough money to stay here longer. I know that sounds bad because I am lucky to be able to go to Hawaii every year. It's just no one is mean here. We can be playing volleyball and a group of people will ask if they can join us, and it would be like we had known them from before.

"Are you ready to go?" Austin asked from the door.

"I guess so," I told him and walked out of my room. We walked out of the condo and headed for the airport.

Chapter 10
Rumor

Once we got back we only had a couple of days until school started. I spent most of my time reading and making sure I had finished all of my homework that I had gotten on the last day before the break. I didn't have too much, but I wanted to make sure what was assigned was finished. It was so I had a few chill days before school started. On Sunday, I went to bed early so I was ready for school the next day.

When I got out of bed the next day, I didn't feel like going to school. I knew I had to though, so I dragged myself out of bed and got dressed. I ate a bowl of cereal and then went to the bathroom to get ready.

"Morning," Austin said when I walked out of the bathroom.

"Morning," I said back.

"Are you ready to go?" he asked me.

"Yep," I told him. I grabbed my backpack and put some shoes on. Then we walked out to the car.

"I might be a little late after school today," he said when he started the car. "Not supper late. Like I will still be able to drive you home, but I have a football meeting in 6th period, and it might run a couple minutes late."

"Okay sounds good," I told him. "Thanks for letting me know." We didn't talk much the rest of the drive. I don't really know why. Maybe because we both didn't want to go to school. I was really dreading seeing Beth again. I don't really want to know what she has to say about me.

When Austin and I walked into school I couldn't help but feel like everyone was looking at me. Maybe I am just being dramatic, but I am pretty sure I heard literal conversations stop. I looked up at my brother, and he must have been feeling the same thing because he was already looking at me. Once I got to my locker, three people I barely talked to were standing next to my locker.

"Hi Nicole," Tami, a girl in my math class, started. "I just wanted to tell you that I am sorry that you have such bad social anxiety. If you want to hangout with someone, you can hang out with me and my friends sometime."

"Wait, what are you talking about?" I questioned.

"Oh well Beth said that when you guys were still friends, you never wanted to do anything because you had really bad anxiety," she informed me.
"What else did she say?" I asked. I was close to crying, but I wasn't going to. My brother wasn't here. He went to his locker, and I don't want to seem like I can't do anything without him.

"Well she said that she thinks it's getting really bad and that you won't talk to anyone but your family because you're terrified. I don't really know why you would have social anxiety, I mean the rest of your family is pretty social. Anyway I just wanted to offer, because she said that your family is probably getting tired of hanging out with you and probably wants to hang out with their actual friends," she told me.

"But the four of us are good friends," I told her.

"See that's why Beth thinks no one will hang out with you. You think your family is your friends. She also said that no one should be friends with you, because you are boring and always scared to do anything fun," she said to me,

"How many people has she told this to?" I asked.

"Oh everyone in the school knows," Sidney, one of Tami's friends, started. "You know everyone thought that you really were friends with your family, but then Beth told us that you only hung out with them because you were scared to talk to anyone else."

"Oh, thanks for telling me I guess," I said, and then they left. I threw my stuff in my locker and went straight for my brother's locker. Callie and Justin were already there.

"You guys heard?" I asked.

"Amy told me," Callie said.

I heard from Alex," Justin joined.

"And I heard from one of my teammates," Austin finished. I let a tear slip. Tami wasn't exaggerating when she said the whole school knew.

"What do I do?" I asked.

"Try not to let it bother you. We're in high school. Within a week something else will happen and the buzz will die down. By the time we are halfway through the second week it will be like nothing ever happened," Callie tried to reassure me.

"Okay but what do I do, because I don't think I will be able to handle everyone staring and feeling sorry for me and laughing all at the same time," I told them.

"Just try and make it through today," Justin said.

"Yeah, we will figure something out after we see how today goes," Austin chimed in.

"Okay I think I can do that," I said. The first bell rang, and I went to my class. It felt like the room went silent when I walked in. I could already tell that this was going to be a long day.

The rest of the day was terrible. All of the people looking at me throughout the day was horrifying. I haven't felt this way since the cafeteria incident last year and even then I felt a little less watched. It was one of the worst days of my life. When the day was finally over, I stood next to my brother's car waiting for him to finish his meeting. There weren't too many people in the parking lot, which I was eternally grateful for. I kept my eyes glued to the door waiting for him to walk out and as soon as he did he unlocked the car for me. I hopped in, and I was lucky enough to get in before any of his teammates tried to ask me a question.

"So how did it go?" he asked me as soon as he got in the car.

"Not great," I told him. "Everyone's eyes were on me all day, and I felt like I was being watched by a bunch of hawks. I didn't run into Beth today though so that's good."

"We'll figure out what to do about the hawk situation," he told me. I nodded. I know they all think that it will die down, and as much as it was hard to believe, I sure hoped they were right.

Chapter 11
Parents

One thing people would never tell you about having a closely knit family is how protective everyone is. It's like everyone in the family, parents, siblings, grandparents, cousins, aunties, and uncles all care so much that it feels good, but can also feel overwhelming. Depending on what it is, I don't like the whole family to know about it. Sometimes I don't want anyone to know about it. After carefully thinking about it, I had decided not to tell my parents about what was going on.

"How was your day?" my mom asked when she got home from work.

"Good!" I said from the living room. My brother, who was sitting across from me, looked right at me.

"You should tell her," he mouthed. I shook my head at him. He gave me the look he always does when he doesn't agree with me, but he didn't push me to say anything else.

"So I was thinking we could just order a pizza for dinner. What do you guys think?" Mom asked. We gave her a look. She never wants to order pizza…or anything really.

"Are you feeling okay?" Austin asked her.
"Yes, I'm feeling fine," Mom responded.

"Then what's up, because if it was up to you, we would never order any food?" I asked her.

"Yes we would!" she argued.

"Mom," we both said.

"Okay fine! It was my turn to get groceries, and I thought we would have enough until tomorrow but we literally have nothing for supper!" she caved. I laughed and so did Austin. "What?"

"A couple weeks ago you got so mad at dad for thinking the exact same thing," I told her, still laughing.

"It was the dumbest fight you guys have ever had!" Austin added.

"I know!" Mom exclaimed. "Please don't tell him!"

"I mean we won't, but I can't promise he won't be suspicious that you of all people ordered pizza," I told her.

"Can't we just say you guys order it before I get home?" she pleaded.
"I mean I guess, but he isn't allowed to get mad at us," Austin said.

"I will make sure he doesn't get mad," Mom said and then she went to order a pizza. It was a weird sight seeing her order a pizza. After the crazy day I've had though, it was nice to laugh.

Dad got home about ten minutes after the pizza arrived. He walked into the kitchen to see the three of us sitting at the table around a big box of pepperoni pizza.

"Hey guy-," he started. "What happened? Why are we eating pizza?"

"The kids ordered it before I got home, but I guess it's okay for a day," my mom blurted, giving him almost no time to finish. I was holding back a laugh, and so was my brother.

"Okay then," my dad said, as he sat down. We all ate the pizza, and it was pretty quiet. The combination of me not wanting to tell them something, my brother thinking I probably should, my mom not enjoying the fact that she ordered pizza, and my dad being confused as to why we were all eating pizza made little room for anyone to have a conversation.

A whole week had passed since the rumors had started, and I had managed to avoid telling my parents this whole time. The rumors are still flying high, but there is not much more that I can do about it. I have tried telling Beth to stop but that obviously didn't work. I fell asleep thinking about that attempt.

It was Wednesday morning, and I was tired of people looking at me like I can't talk to anyone. I knew it was a long shot talking to Beth, but at this point I was desperate. I walked into the school quickly, and I hadn't even realized that my brother was tailing me the whole way to the cafeteria. I saw her sitting there with her boyfriend, and I walked up to the two of them.

"Beth, I need to talk to you," I said standing across the table.

"Why?" she asked me.

"Look I don't know why you decided to make something up about the social anxiety that I don't have-," I started.

"I didn't make it up. You definitely do have social anxiety seeing as you talk to three people," she argued.

"No I don't and definitely not in the way you made it seem!" I exclaimed.

"But I mean you kind of do. You don't talk to anyone and after one friendship gone wrong you revert to only talking to your family. You sit alone at parties, you-"

"Okay enough," my brother interrupted. He must have noticed I was shaking.

Why should she?" James asked. "Nicole is the one who came up to us when we had no intention of bothering her and all Beth is saying is the truth."

"No intention of bothering her. You guys have made her life miserable for almost two years and you couldn't stop, so you started a dumb rumor about her!" my brother argued. I couldn't do this anymore. It felt the same way it did last year, the last fight, the same room, same people. I looked up at my brother and he had the same look of anger that he had last year. The only thing that was different was that Callie and Justin weren't here. I'm sure they would be though, if they knew where we were.

"Hey Nicole, are you going to let your brother and my boyfriend get into a fight again?" Beth asked me.

"What? No!" I replied.

"You sure? Because we are only a couple sentences and an insult away from that happening," she told me.

"You need to mind your own business!" my brother yelled. There weren't many people in the cafeteria but the ones who were there were staring.

"Hey don't yell at her!" James shouted at my brother. I was so done with this. It was probably my dumbest idea since I decided to become friends with the girl sitting across the table from me.

"Let's just go. It was worth a shot," I looked up at my brother pleadingly.

"Okay," he hesitated. "Yeah, let's go." We walked out of the cafeteria, and just like that it was over. That was so close to being another suspension for my brother, and that could have probably jeopardized his possible scholarships, and his future would have been jeopardized because of me. The weirdest part though was, within a second, all of the fighting just ended. You walk out of a room, and it's done. It's too bad I didn't have the guts to walk out before the pop was dumped on me, before my brother was punching James, before Callie was screaming, and before Justin was holding James back and taking the opening chance to take a hit at him. It's weird that everytime I see her, the same pit in my stomach, the same guilt comes rushing back. Even when I approach her, she still has the upper hand.

When I woke up it was already 10:30 Saturday morning. I am not usually one to sleep past nine thirty, but it has been a really long week. I changed out of my pajamas and I heard Callie's voice, and then I heard Justin's. They are usually not here this early on the weekends, and we didn't plan to meet up to do anything until tomorrow. I moved quickly down the stairs still trying to figure out what they were doing here.
"We're really worried about her," I heard Callie say. I was standing in the entrance, but I was quiet enough for them not to notice me.

"Yeah, Wednesday was really bad," Austin added. *Why are they talking about me? Wait,* I thought. *They are telling my parents!*

"I just really hope she doesn't feel as terrible as she did last year," Justin said sympathetically.

"This is the second time something has happened that she hasn't told us," my mom said.

"I didn't tell you because it's not a big deal," I said. They all whipped their heads around, shocked that I had heard, mad I didn't tell.

"I'd say a rumor that affects you this badly is a pretty big deal," my dad told me.

"It's not though," I started. "They all said they think it's going to die down," I finished, pointing at the three of them.

"That was before it had been a week and nothing changed, before Wednesday, before it continuously affects you whether you admit it or not," Callie argued.

"After they told us all of this, we've been thinking," my mom said to me. "You may not have social anxiety the way that Beth makes it seem, but on one level or another you have some. We thought maybe going to a counselor to help you with coping skills might help you a bit. We also thought it would be good to tell the principal about what is going on."

"No, to all of that," I replied.

"Why won't you even consider it?" my dad questioned.

"Because a counselor isn't going to be any help at all. She can't make the rumor go away and that is the only way I will be able to feel less anxious and no coping skills will help me with that. If you go to the principal, that not only won't make the rumors stop but will give them a second thing to talk about."

"But maybe they will be able to help you and you can't see it yet," My mom insisted.

"They won't though! No one can help me. Not even the people in this room will be able to help me, because no one knows what I'm going through," I turned to face Austin, Callie, and Justin. "Guys I appreciate your help through it all, but there is nothing more you can do and if you keep protecting me, soon enough it has a chance of jeopardizing your future and holds the possibility of making my situation worse."

"But we really want to be able to help you," Austin countered.

"No! I don't need protection! I love you all to death, but I need to be able to do some stuff alone. I can't rely on you to step in whenever it becomes too much. I need to be able to do that on my own and the only way to do that is if I don't have you guys ready to jump in all the time!" I shouted and then I walked away and bolted up the stairs.

Chapter 12
Regret

Do I feel terrible and regret what I said three days ago? Yes. There is no excusing what I said to my brother and cousins who in the long run were just trying to help. They know it, and I know it. Even though what I said was completely terrible, there was a sense of truth in the things I had said: I need to learn how to stand up for myself. I never needed to stand up for myself before, and it makes me an easy target for anyone who wants to pick on me, including Beth. I don't know how to stand up to people though. Everytime I try, it's like I am getting walked all over.

We get to the middle of the next week, and the only people that are talking to me are my parents. I think the reason they are talking to me is because they are my parents and they feel bad for me. I don't get rides from Austin; my mom drives me instead. Austin goes and picks up Callie and Justin now, and I am pretty sure he only does it to get out of the house sooner. He either goes to their house or a friend's after school and will only come home right before supper. Callie hasn't responded to any of my texts or phone calls and won't look at me in the halls. Justin seems to be doing his best to avoid me at all costs, because I haven't even seen him that much and he won't pick up a single call. It's safe to say that they are all furious with me, but I don't think I can blame them.

I was walking through the hallway alone again, and it was now Thursday. I saw the three of them walking, and they saw me.
"Hi," I started. They breezed by me, and no one bothered to engage in conversation. I watched them walk away. I saw my brother turn his head and then he looked back to the front. They don't even want to hear me out. That hurt quite a bit, because I know what I did, but it's not like they have never done things. Like the time Callie lied and said she was sick instead of just being honest and said she had already had plans. I wouldn't have cared if she had told me the truth, but it bothered me that she lied and I still forgave her. I get that I messed up. I really do, but if they would just give me a chance.

Chapter 13
102 unread messages

102. Between the three of them I had messaged them 102 times. That doesn't even include the many, many calls I have made. I might sound desperate, but I don't care. I am. I need to be able to talk to them again, and I don't think I can handle the silence whenever we are in the same room anymore.

It's Saturday, and I finally came up with a great plan. I am going to send a message to all of them. Hopefully sending a group message to meet up for dinner will spark some interest. Then I am going to pray that they will stay long enough to hear my apology. I thought a while about what to send them and then it was sent:

> "Hey guys. I know I messed up big time. Can we meet for dinner so I can apologize face to face? I will buy it and you can order whatever you want from any restaurant. I just want you to hear me out. I'm sorry."

I set my phone down with the screen facing the bed and then I paced around the room. If they say no I have no idea what to do. I think if I say no that's it, there will be nothing left for me to do. I would just have to accept the fact that they will be mad at me forever. My phone buzzing snapped me out of it. Two new messages, Justin was the first to respond:

> "What time?" he asked.
> Callie was close behind him:
> "Pizza?"
> "5:30 and pizza sounds great," I answered.

It was almost five thirty, and my brother still hadn't responded. If he wasn't with them, I didn't think he would be coming. I guess I can't blame him. All he wanted to do was help. All he ever wants to do is help. It's gotten him in trouble before, just like it did a year ago, but it is also probably why he has made so many friends. I have never met one person that has doubted his loyalty. Not one teammate, friend, family member, not even me. He would never intentionally hurt anyone. I didn't intentionally hurt him either, but I did. I wonder if he knows that the look he gave me the day after when we were all sat at the dinner table almost destroyed me?

It was a day after I had gotten mad at everyone. I hadn't seen my brother all day. He left before I was awake. He had to eventually come home for supper. My family wouldn't let him skip supper because we were in a fight. There were only two reasons you could miss supper:
1. You had plans at least a week in advance.
2. Something for school or sports teams.

My parents said it was because supper time is important to a family. That we should all be able to get together at least once a day so we don't become one of those families who never talk to each other. The hope is that when me and my brother move out of the house we will all still stay in touch. Seems odd to me, but I would never say something to my parents about it. He walked in when I was sitting at the table. Mom and dad were still in the kitchen. He sat across from me and made sure not to look me in the eyes. I looked down at my plate and when I looked back up he was staring daggers at me. No guilt, no sadness, no pain, nothing but pure anger. He wouldn't break eye contact when I made it. I didn't know what to do. I knew he could see the guilt in my face, but I didn't want to break eye contact. It hurt so much to see how mad he was at me, so much so that I looked back down to hide the fact that I had shed a tear. I don't know if he knows how important he is to me, but if he did he would also know how much he had hurt me then and how much the silence every time we are in the same room makes me want to run into my room and hide from the world.

The sound of a car pulling up snapped me out of my thoughts. I looked out of the window, and it was Austin's! I let out a sigh of relief. In the long run he showed up. I knew he was here for this, because Justin was in the passenger seat and Callie in the back. Justin and Callie got out quickly, but I saw my brother hesitate. Callie opened his door and must have said something to convince him to get out of the car, because he unbuckled his seat belt and got out of his car. I had bought three large pizzas, one pepperoni, one with a bunch of different meats and one buffalo pizza. We all eat all three of these kinds, and we eat a lot of pizza. Mom and Dad weren't home. They were going on a weekend trip, but that really means they went to a hotel in town to get away from the chaos of our home. I decided it would be best to wait at the kitchen table in my spot waiting for them to show up.

I heard the door open and their voices silently whispering to each other. Justin was the first one to pop their head around the corner.

"Top three?" he asked. I nodded with a soft smile. I didn't realize that even a simple question like that could make me feel terrible about what I did all over again. A simple reminder that if this goes up in flames, I lose the most important people in my life. It wouldn't matter if they eventually forgave me. The dynamic would have completely changed, and we would become one of those families that don't always get together and only see each other at family gatherings.

"Do you have something that we can drink?" Callie asked, as she came around the corner. It took me a minute to realize she had asked a question that required me to verbally answer.

Umm yeah," I finally answered. "There are a couple kinds of pop, apple juice, and water in the fridge."

"Okay," she said as she made her way to the fridge.

"Can you get me some water?" my brother asked her as he made his way to the kitchen.

"Yep," she responded. Justin sat to the right of me and my brother sat across from him. When Callie came back, she sat across from me. An awkward silence filled the room as I built up the courage to speak up. I mean they're here, so that means there is a part of them that wants to hear me out.

"So in case you didn't notice from the many messages and phone calls, I wanted to apologize. I am well aware that what I said that day was wrong, and I should never have said those things to you. I didn't mean any of it, but that said some of it was true. I have had a lot of time to reflect and you guys are the most important people to me, and I would hate it if you were mad at me forever, but I also need to learn how to stand up for myself. I think if I can't, I will just keep being a target, and it could affect you guys. I should have said it like that from the start, and I shouldn't have had a hint of meanness and I shouldn't have yelled. I'm really, really sorry." The last part came out kind of shaky. I had said what I could and now it was up to them. We sat there for a minute in dead silence. It's like they didn't know how to answer.

"Okay, I forgive you," Austin finally spoke up. Callie and Justin both nodded. Just like that, this weight that I had been carrying around since those words had left my mouth that day was gone, and I felt better about life.

"Can we eat now?" Justin asked, looking pleadingly.

Yeah," I said with a little laugh. I looked at my brother, and he smiled. It was the first time he had smiled at me in what felt like forever.

Callie and Justin had to leave about an hour after we were done eating. They had to go and help their parents set up for a gathering for her mom's college the next day. We said goodbye, and then Austin and I headed for the living room.

"So now that we are talking again, can I ask you something?" I questioned.

"Yeah, what's up?" he replied.

"Well I was just wondering if you had thought about your football offerings anymore?" I asked.

"Actually I have. I have to decide which school, but I know I want to follow through with one. I thought about it and all of the offers I got are verbal which means none of them are official. I just feel like I am a lot closer to dad when I play the sport, and I don't really think I am ready to leave football in the past," I smiled at him. It was nice to hear that he wanted to keep playing.

"That's good to hear. When are you going to tell mom and dad?" I questioned.

"I actually told them yesterday when you were in your room. Hey, you want to go for a drive?"

"Sure!" I answered. Then he tossed me the keys.

"Wait really?" I asked.
"Well yeah! You have had your learners for so long, and you haven't gone driving since the beginning of the school year. You need to start practicing so when you turn sixteen you feel ready."

"What do you mean I haven't gone driving?"

"Going for 5 minutes around the block once a weekend with dad isn't going to cut it when you want to be able to take your test and pass."

"Fair," I said.

"Okay, let's go!" he told me. I got up off the couch and put my shoes on. I walked out of the house and into the driver's seat of my brother's car. I got to pick the music, because he said it would make me feel a little bit less nervous if I was listening to something I actually liked. The first five minutes were the worst. My hands were shaking, and I had to have an extra tight grip on the steering wheel, but then I got used to it and I think I got better. My brother didn't make me feel terrible about my driving skills either, so that made me feel a little bit better. It was nice to be able to talk to him again.

Chapter 14
Stand Up

By the time Monday came, I had kind of forgotten about all of the rumors with all of the craziness of the weekend. That is until I walked into the building and everyone was looking at me. Some started with sympathy, some with the clear thought that I was dramatic, and some with confusion. Either way, the pure idea of people still looking at me sent an uneasy chill down my spine. To put a cherry on top of this great day, Beth was standing next to my locker.

"Hey Nicole, nice to see you and your family getting along again. It's still sad though, them being your only friends, I mean," she said.

"It's not sad Beth," I started.

"Umm, yeah, yeah it is," she interrupted.

"Look Beth. I need you to leave me alone, and I need you to figure out a way to stop these rumors," I said, a little shaky at first but the second part was more confident.

"Why would I do that?"

"Because I told you to, and if you had any little bit of human decency you would listen and respect that," I answered.

"That is the dumbest thing I have ever heard," she laughed slightly. "You know all of this stuff that I know about is because of you. It's your fault that you gave me all of that info on you."

"It is not my fault that I trusted someone who I had known for years, because we had always been in the same class and had been friends for a year and a half," I told her.

"See thats why I know the rumors I started aren't all lies, because if you were social you would know that you don't tell everything to someone and you don't tell anything you don't want a lot of people to know because you have no idea what they are going to do with that information."

"That still doesn't make it my fault that you chose to go behind my back," I was nervous that she would win this and that I wouldn't have the guts to do this again.

"Again it kind of does," she said. This sudden rush of confidence came through me.

"Look Beth, I am done with you and your boyfriend trying to hurt me. I don't know what happened to you that made you like this, but if I did I wouldn't tell the whole school about it because I have the little bit of common sense that is required to know that it would hurt someone. I have been doing some reading about insecurities, and you have just as many insecurities as I have. We just show them differently and hurt people, hurt people. To fully detach myself from you, I have to forgive you. So I forgive you, Beth, for all of the hurtful things you have said and done to me. You don't have control over me and my feelings anymore. I am taking control of my life and who is allowed in it. I wish you well, and there is one last thing you can do for me - I need you to make these rumors go away," I finished. I didn't even really know what I had said or where it came from, but I am glad I said it because I saw a look of surprise flash across her face.

"Rumors don't just go away you know. It's out in the universe, and I can't just stop people from talking. It doesn't work like that," she countered.

"Well then do your best. If you care about apologizing at all then you will make an effort to at least make my life a little less miserable," I finished the argument, and she stopped trying to argue. I think I finally shut her up, and I think there's a chance she will leave me alone because she walked away from my locker. I put my stuff into my locker and went over to my family.

"Hey how did it go?" Austin asked me. I had told him my plan in the car on the way there.

"How did what go?" Callie questioned.

"I kind of just stood up to Beth on my own, and I think it worked. Like I don't think she will bother me anymore," I answered.

"Wait really?" Justin asked, kind of surprised and kind of happy.

"Yeah!" I exclaimed. Callie hugged me and Austin and Justin smiled. I smiled too. I finally stood up to Beth on my own! Whether she understood and will actually leave me alone is a different story but now I know I could do it again. I saw Beth talking to a bunch of different people, bouncing from group to group. I don't know if it was positive or negative or if it had anything to do with me at all, but I didn't care.

Chapter 15
Summer

It didn't take long before I felt like the rumors died down. I don't know if it was because Beth helped them die down, if they died down on their own, or if I just got used to it but it wasn't bothering me anymore. It felt really good to end the year on a high note, or at least not a bad one. We obviously had to write finals, and they went surprisingly well. Both Austin and I got high 80s on most of our tests which we found really surprising. Justin got high 90s on every single one of his tests which didn't surprise me. I know it's a really high mark and it probably should have surprised me, but I have spent years watching him get close to, if not perfect scores on his tests and projects. Callie definitely didn't fail any of her finals but you could tell which subjects she was strong in. It was done though; the school year was over.

You know that feeling you get when summer is starting? You realize that you don't have to hang out with anyone you don't want to see. The sun is out for longer, nights get later and so does the time you get up. Most importantly, you get to do what you want to do and don't have to be on any sort of schedule. One of the best parts of summer though is the lake. Justin and Callie don't have a cabin, but they come out to ours quite a bit. It's my second favorite place in the world (right after Hawaii). Austin and I spend almost every day of the summer at the lake, and our parents come when they are done working. They usually spend the night, but sometimes they have to get up earlier so they spend the night at home.

It was only Austin and I at the cabin today. It was pretty hot outside, but I went out to sit on our dock for a bit. It was early in the morning, but there were still boats on the lake. There was a group of maybe ten year olds tubing, and I could hear one girl screaming when I was extremely far away from them. It was pretty funny, because I am willing to bet that the other girls loved going fast and thought it was funny that she was screaming. It was how we were when Callie went tubing for the first time. There were a couple of people on paddle boards and the blonde lady must have said something funny because the brunette was laughing. I heard footsteps on the dock.

"You want to go practice driving for a bit?" Austin asked me. "You will be able to take your test in a month, so you should practice as much as you can."

"Yeah sure," I said standing up. We walked off the dock, through the cabin, and to Austin's car. I got pretty used to driving with Austin. I got quite a bit better at driving, because we have been practicing a lot recently. I drove all around the area. It was a pretty big area, so I got a lot of practice. Then I drove back to the cabin. I pulled up and Justin's car was in the driveway. The two of them were sitting on the step. I got out of the car and closed the door. Once Austin was out I gave him his keys.

"Hey guys!" Callie said standing up.

"Hey!" I replied. "I didn't know you were coming today."
"Yeah we didn't have much to do, so we thought we should come and see what you were up to," Justin told Austin and me.

"Great! What do you guys want to do?" Austin asked.

We could go for a swim," I suggested.

"Yes!" Callie exclaimed.

"Wait, did you guys bring your bathing suits?" Austin questioned. "Because we could walk to the old restaurant and have an early lunch if you didn't."

"Of course we brought our bathing suits. We are at the lake," Justin replied.

"Yeah, but you never know what you guys might forget," my brother said. We all laughed. They went out to grab their bags from the car and then we all went to separate rooms and changed. Once we had all finished we went outside and started walking into the water. It was pretty cold, and it took me a while to get used to it. The rocks on the bottom of the lake were pretty smooth to the point where it felt like I was walking on a flat surface, but every so often there would be a rock out of place that would catch me off guard. We went out far but were careful not to pass the buoys. We had lots of laughs and lots of splashes that morning, and when I saw the three of them smiling I realized something. For the first time in a long time I wasn't stressing about what people thought of me. I wasn't worried someone was going to make fun of me. I wasn't spending a lot of nights crying when I was alone and no one could hear. I realized I was happy with my brother and our cousins. I realized that for the first time in what felt like forever, nothing was bothering me. Maybe one day I will find it easier to talk to more people and it's probably something I should work at, but right now I am okay with just talking to my family and working on myself. It's nothing that should bother me, and it's nothing that people should make fun of me for. I'm not worried about anything right now, and I am spending time with people who actually care about me. For the first time in a long time, I can say that I am just happy. I am happy with the person I am and am growing into. Nothing else and no worries in my head. I'm happy.

Halle Harty was fourteen when she decided to write a book. She has had some great teachers who helped develop her writing skills as well as her mom who helped her edit the story. When she isn't in school or writing, she is spending her time in the dance studio or on the volleyball court. She also likes to read, and loves photography, as well as watching TV shows and movies. Her family and friends are very important to her and have always helped her and supported her through all her goals.

Manufactured by Amazon.ca
Bolton, ON

35379117R00042